# A Note to Parents

Your child is beginning the lifelong adventure of reading! And with the **World of Reading** program, you can be sure that he or she is receiving the encouragement needed to become a confident, independent reader. This program is specially designed to encourage your child to enjoy reading at every level by combining exciting, easy-to-read stories featuring favorite characters with colorful art that brings the magic to life.

The **World of Reading** program is divided into four levels so that children at any stage can enjoy a successful reading experience:

## Reader-in-Training
### Pre-K–Kindergarten
Picture reading and word repetition for children who are getting ready to read.

## Beginner Reader
### Pre-K–Grade 1
Simple stories and easy-to-sound-out words for children who are just learning to read.

## Junior Reader
### Kindergarten–Grade 2
Slightly longer stories and more varied sentences perfect for children who are reading with the help of a parent.

## Super Reader
### Grade 1–Grade 3
Encourages independent reading with rich story lines and wide vocabulary that's right for children who are reading on their own.

Learning to read is a once-in-a-lifetime adventure, and with **World of Reading**, the journey is just beginning!

SUSTAINABLE
FORESTRY
INITIATIVE

Certified Chain of Custody
Promoting Sustainable Forestry

www.sfiprogram.org
SFI-01415
The SFI label applies to the text stock

For more Disney Press fun, visit www.disneybooks.com

DISNEY

# MICKEY & FRIENDS

## Donald Takes a Trip

By Kate Ritchey
Illustrated by the Disney Storybook Artists
and Loter, Inc.

DISNEY PRESS
New York

It was a hot summer day.
The sun was shining on
Donald and his friends.

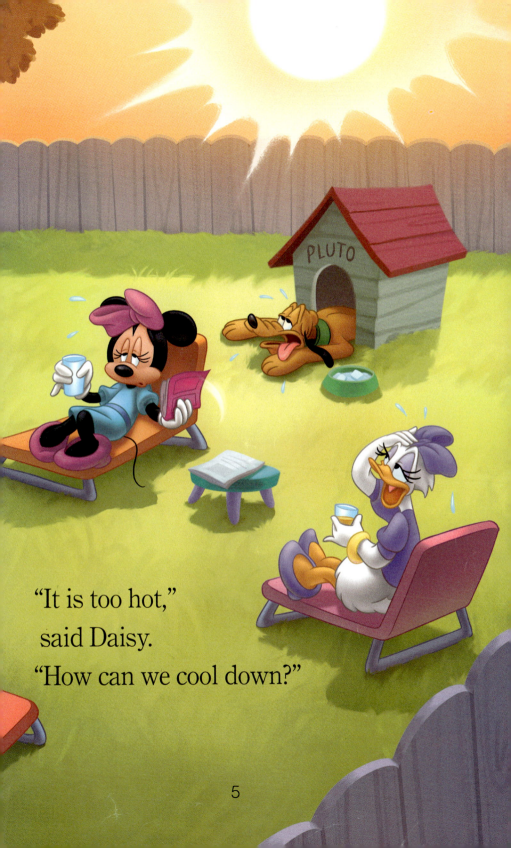

"It is too hot,"
said Daisy.
"How can we cool down?"

"We could go sit
in the shade," said Mickey.
"Maybe we could
find a fan," Minnie said.

"Gosh," said Goofy.
"Those sprinklers look
nice and cool."

Then Donald had an idea.
"I know what we can do,"
he said.
"Let's go to the lake!"

"What a great idea!"
said Mickey.
"It is the perfect day
for a swim," said Daisy.

Donald went home to pack.
There was so much to take!
Swimsuit, beach ball, towel . . .

Donald loved the lake.
His favorite thing to do
was to go fishing.

On the way to the lake,
the friends sang songs
and played games.

When they got
to the lake,
the six friends ran
into the water.

"Ahh," said Donald.
The water felt nice
on the very hot day.

Soon they had cooled off.
"What should we do next?"
Daisy asked her friends.

Minnie wanted to play ball.
Goofy wanted to swim more.
Mickey and Pluto wanted
to play Frisbee.

But Donald had
another idea.
"Come on, everyone!
It is time to go fishing!"

17

"I do not think we can
all fit in the boat,"
said Minnie. "Let's do
something together."

But Donald only wanted
to go fishing.
So he decided to go
all by himself.

Donald rowed out to
the middle of the lake.

He found a good spot
and began to fish.

Donald waited.
And he waited.
But his fishing line
never moved!

Donald was getting upset.
Where were the fish?
Then he heard
a splashing noise. . . .

Donald turned around
and saw a fish!
He heard another splash
and turned again.

The fish kept splashing,
and Donald kept turning.

Soon Donald was
all tangled up!

Just then, Goofy swam by.
"Gosh," Goofy said.
"You look like you
could use some help."

Goofy untangled Donald.
Then he climbed aboard
and the friends
fished together.

Donald was glad
to have Goofy along!
Fishing was more fun
with a friend.

Back on the shore,
the friends built a fire.
They roasted marshmallows.
Goofy told a ghost story.

Soon it was time to go home.

"That was fun!"
Donald said.
"Who wants to go
fishing with me tomorrow?"

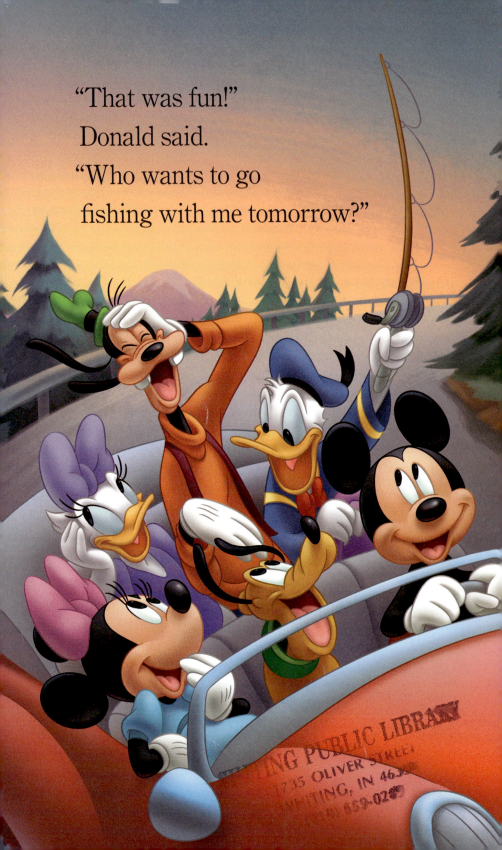